LA JOLLA COUNTRY DAY SCHOOL LIBRARY

3 0365 1000 2681 5

D0570855

DATE DUE			
			PRINTED IN U.S.A.

For Nausicaa
 — *O. W.*

Odile Weulersse is a French author who has written numerous books for children, many of them focused on retelling old legends and stories for a young audience. She lives in France and teaches film at the Sorbonne.

Rébecca Dautremer is a French illustrator who has brought many stories to life with her rich and whimsical art, including *The Secret Lives of Princesses* (Sterling) and *Swing Café* (The Secret Mountain). Visit her website at www.rebeccadautremer.com.

© Flammarion, 2005
87, Panhard et Levassor – 75647 Paris Cedex 13
http://www.editions.flammarion.com

Original Title: *Nasreddine*

All rights reserved

Published in 2013 by Eerdmans Books for Young Readers,
an imprint of Wm. B. Eerdmans Publishing Co.
2140 Oak Industrial Dr. NE
Grand Rapids, Michigan 49505
P.O. Box 163, Cambridge CB3 9PU U.K.

www.eerdmans.com/youngreaders

Manufactured at Tien Wah Press
in Malaysia in October 2012, first printing

19 18 17 16 15 14 13   9 8 7 6 5 4 3 2 1

Library of Congress Cataloging-in-Publication Data

Weulersse, Odile, 1938-
Nasreddine / by Odile Weulersse; illustrated by Rébecca Dautremer;
[translated by Kathleen Merz].
p. cm.
Summary: As Nasreddine and his father take dates, wool, chickens,
or watermelon to market, people tease them no matter who is riding
their donkey, and this causes Nasreddine embarrassment until his
father helps him to understand.
ISBN 978-0-8028-5416-2
[1. Teasing — Fiction. 2. Embarrassment — Fiction. 3. Fathers and
sons — Fiction. 4. Middle East — Fiction.] I. Dautremer, Rébecca, ill.
II. Merz, Kathleen. III. Title.
PZ7.W5355Nas 2013
[E] — dc23
2012025469

FSC
www.fsc.org
MIX
Paper from
responsible sources
FSC® C012700

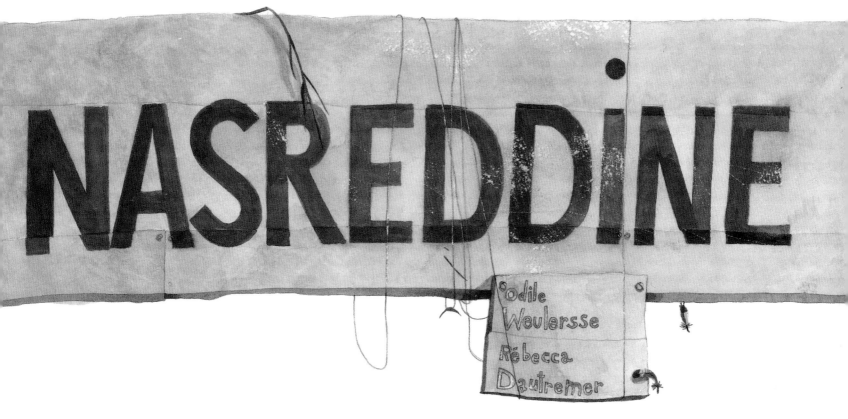

NASREDDINE

Odile
Weulersse

Rébecca
Dautremer

Eerdmans Books for Young Readers

Grand Rapids, Michigan • Cambridge, U.K.

JOLLA COUNTRY DAY SCHOOL
LIBRARY
9490 GENESEE AVENUE
LA JOLLA, CA 92037

One morning, Nasreddine was sitting on a carpet in the shade of a palm, drinking camel's milk with cinnamon, when his father Mustafa called him: "Nasreddine, bring the donkey from the stables. We are going to the market."

"As you wish, Father," the young boy replied, putting on his hat and Turkish slippers.

Nasreddine brought the animal to his father, and together they loaded a large basket of dates onto the donkey's back.

Mustafa rode on the donkey's back, and Nasreddine walked behind.
The path was still muddy from the last rainfall, so the young boy
took off his slippers to keep them from getting dirty.

Near the city gate, Nasreddine and his father met a vizier on a beautiful Arabian horse. When he saw Mustafa, the vizier exclaimed to his followers: "Look what we have here! A lazy man who lounges and makes his son slosh through the mud!"

Mustafa calmly answered: "Your words, sir, are hurting my ears."

But Nasreddine turned red. His heart was full of shame that these people would dare to make fun of them.

"I'm going home," he declared. "I'm tired."

"Already?" said Mustafa.

"Yes, then no one will make fun of us anymore."

His father laughed and said, "As you wish, my son."

The following week, Nasreddine sheared wool from the sheep, who had been suffering from the heat ever since spring had come. The sheep wiggled to avoid the burn of the razor, but the boy was careful not to hurt their soft pink skin.

When he finished, Nasreddine gathered the balls of wool in a huge sack. His father came over and said: "You've done a good job, my son. Go find the donkey, and let's take the wool to the weavers."

"As you wish, Father."

When he came back with the animal,
Nasreddine was limping.

"I twisted my ankle," he explained.

"Just now? Walking through the yard?"

"Yes," Nasreddine said, looking at his feet.

Mustafa smiled knowingly. "Well, if it hurts
to walk, then you'd better climb up on
the donkey."

Nasreddine took the bottom of his robe
in his mouth and scrambled up onto
the donkey, pleased with his trick —
no one would make fun of his father
walking calmly behind, his head
wrapped in a handsome turban.

The road was rocky along the river, and the women washing their clothes turned around at the sound of the hooves. As Nasreddine and his father passed, the women regarded them gravely.

"Look how the world works these days! The children ride, and their elders walk behind. Fathers don't have any authority at all."

"You're right," said another. "No one respects older folks anymore."

"As if the two of them couldn't ride together on the donkey," a third added.

Mustafa remained calm and answered them firmly:
"Your words, women, are hurting my ears."

But Nasreddine turned red and, a little later,
slipped to the ground. "I'm going to go back to
the house — I forgot to close the sheep pen!"

"You don't have a twisted ankle anymore?"

"No, no — it healed all by itself."

"Well, do as you wish."

A few days later Nasreddine was chasing a hen in the poultry yard. She ran away on her short legs, flapping her wings and clucking, trying to escape.

Nasreddine grabbed her by the neck and shut her in a wooden cage.

"My pretty, my beautiful, you're going to take a long trip to the market. I'll bring you some company so that you don't get bored."

On tiptoe, he approached another plump hen.

After filling the cage with five hens and a rooster, he steered the cage toward the house, where his father was waiting.

"It's very hot today," said Nasreddine. "It will be tiring to walk. Let's both ride on the donkey."

Mustafa smiled mischievously. "As you wish, my son."

Once again the donkey traveled down the road, this time carrying on its back the son and the father, as well as the five hens and the rooster in their cage.

At the marketplace, there were a few old men drinking frozen lemonade at a table outside a café. The clucking of the hens caught their attention. One man chuckled, his neighbor snorted, and then the whole group roared with laughter as the donkey passed, carrying the son, the father, the hens, and the rooster.

"Look at that cruel man tormenting his animal. Poor animal — its belly is almost touching the ground!" one man exclaimed.

"The boy is sitting so far forward, he's breaking its neck," another remarked.

"That donkey will die from exhaustion in this heat. Some people can be so horrible to their animals!"

"Be quiet, you old fools. Your words are hurting my ears," Mustafa said calmly, and they continued on their way.

As soon as they were out of sight of the old men, Nasreddine started squirming on the donkey.

"What's the matter?" his father asked.

"I have pins and needles in my behind. It might be better if I get down and go back home."

"Pins and needles? From riding a donkey? That's rare," his father remarked, smiling. "But if that's what you want, then do as you wish."

The following week, Nasreddine thought he had found the perfect solution.

"The donkey is tired," he said, dragging a huge bag of watermelons. "He looked unhappy this morning and wouldn't eat the grass I gave him."

"How are we going to get our fruit to the market?" asked his father innocently.

Embarrassed, Nasreddine suggested: "We could walk behind the donkey, and that way he would only have to carry the watermelons. That would be lighter."

"That is an excellent idea, my son," said Mustafa with a mischievous smile.

With such a light load, the donkey trotted quickly —
so quickly that Mustafa and Nasreddine had trouble
keeping up.

Along the way, a little boy started following them,
laughing. A little while later, a second boy joined the
first — then another, and another. Soon there was
a small group amusing themselves by watching the
donkey and its owners.

"Why are they laughing at us?" Nasreddine asked
his father.

"At their age, you make fun of everything," Mustafa
responded in his calm voice. "Let's keep going."

But a little girl said loudly: "Why do those two prefer to tire themselves out rather than tire out their donkey?"

"Because they are stupid!" answered the boys.

Nasreddine felt his heart sink down to his feet. He turned as red as a pepper and ran away.

For several days, Nasreddine thought.

When market day arrived again, Nasreddine brought the donkey to his father and said: "Father, I've found a way for us to go to market without anyone making fun of us. We can carry the donkey."

Mustafa smiled.

"Where is your common sense, my son? Your suggestion is ridiculous. I've let you do as you wish until now, but today you need to understand your mistake."

"I haven't made a mistake. I've listened to everyone!"

"That's exactly your mistake. People can always find a reason to criticize you if they want to. So, what do you think we should do?"

"Not listen to them?" mumbled Nasreddine, so confused that tears sprang to his eyes.

"Exactly. It's up to you to decide if what you're hearing is wise, or if it's only a silly and hurtful remark."

Nasreddine looked up at his father and declared triumphantly: "I understand! You can't be afraid that other people will judge you or make fun of you."

Mustafa smiled warmly. "I am happy that my son, the jewel of my heart, knows how to reason so well."

Historical Note

Stories about Nasreddine
are told throughout the Middle East
and beyond. They are often said to be based
on a real man who lived in Turkey during the
Middle Ages. The stories have been changed
and added to over the years, but
Nasreddine has never lost
his ability to offer both
wisdom and delight.